by
Carolyn Crimi

Tessa's Tip-Tapping Toes

illustrated by
Marsha Gray
Carrington

Orchard Books • New York

An Imprint of Scholastic Inc.

Book design by Nancy Goldenberg
The text of this book is set in 14 point Hiroshige Medium.
The illustrations are acrylic.

10 9 8 7 6 5 4 3 2 1 02 03 04 05

Printed in Mexico 49
First edition, March 2002

Library of Congress Cataloging-in-Publication Data
Crimi, Carolyn.
Tessa's tip-tapping toes / by Carolyn Crimi ; illustrated by Marsha Gray Carrington.
—1st ed.   p.   cm.
Summary: Inspired by the rhythm of the rain, a mouse that loves to dance and a cat
with a penchant for singing find that they can no longer control their impulses.
ISBN 0-439-31768-1 (alk. paper)
[1. Mice—Fiction. 2. Cats—Fiction. 3. Singing—Fiction. 4. Dance—Fiction.]
I. Carrington, Marsha Gray, ill. II. Title.
PZ7.C86928 Te 2002
[E]—dc21   2001034003

For my nieces and nephews—Katelyn, Justin, Dorothy, Robert, Max, Olivia, and Jack.

With special thanks to Cynthia Leitich Smith, who helped Tessa dance.—C.C.

For my mom,
a constant source of creative inspiration,
and my dad, an endless source of
kid inspiration.
I love you. —M.G.C.

Tessa had swinging arms, skipping feet,
and tip-tapping toes. She was built to dance.

Most mice scurried along
floorboards and ledges,
trying not to be seen.
Not Tessa.

She boogied, she bopped,

she shimmied, she hopped,

she flounced and she bounced, but she never scurried.

"Tessa! Stop twirling so!" her mother would scold.

Tessa would try to stop with every ounce of her be-boppin', hip-hoppin' heart. But when her toes weren't tip-tapping, they felt all wrong.

At night Tessa and her family raided Mrs. Timboni's
kitchen, hunting for crumbs. But instead of hurrying
and scurrying, Tessa juggled jelly beans and sashayed
with saltshakers. She loved to tap-dance across the
teapot, wearing her bottle-cap slippers.

P

S

Clickity-clack-clack, Tessa danced.

Then one day Mrs. Timboni got a cat.
His name was Oscar, and his head was
filled with songs.

Most cats liked dozing on windowsills
or curling up on fresh piles of laundry.

Not Oscar. He crooned on the kitchen counters,

sang in the sinks,

and trilled on the dining room table.

"Oscar! Stop all that racket!" cried Mrs. Timboni. "What will the neighbors think!"

Oscar tried stopping with every ounce of his singsongy humdinger of a heart. But when his tongue wasn't trilling, he felt all wrong.

As soon as Tessa's mother heard Oscar's
crooning, she worried that the new cat would
catch her dancing daughter.

"You must be more careful!" she told Tessa. "No more
bounding! No leaping! No spinning! From now on you will
scamper and scurry like a proper mouse!"

So Tessa hurried and scurried. She skittered and scampered.
She stayed low to the ground and didn't make a sound.

But it was hard, so hard. When she
heard Oscar's songs, Tessa bit her tail to
keep herself from dancing.

Within a week the neighbors complained about Oscar. Mrs. Timboni worried that they would ask her to get rid of her chorusing kitty.

"You must be more careful!" she told Oscar. "No more singing! No crooning or caterwauling! From now on you will nap and chase mice like a proper cat!"

So Oscar napped until noon and dozed right through dinner. At night he chased the hurrying, scurrying mice back into their holes.

But it was hard, so hard. When he heard the skitter-scamper of little mice feet, Oscar bit his tongue to keep himself from singing.

Then spring came.

Dozens of daffodils danced in the yard, and green leaves rustled in the breeze.

Tessa watched the daffodils sway. She longed to dance, but she remembered her mother's warning and kept still.

Oscar listened to the leaves swish. He longed to sing, but he remembered Mrs. Timboni's warning and kept silent.

Until one night when Oscar was awakened by the *ting, ting, ting* of rain on the roof.

Oscar's tongue twitched. His throat throbbed. His teeth chattered and his lips quivered. Before he knew it, a song sprang out of his mouth.

"Doo-Whappa-Whappa Doo-Whappa-Whappa!" he sang. *"Doo-Lang-Doo Lang-Doo-Lang . . ."*

Doo-Whappa-Whappa

CAT NAP

Doo-Whappa-Whappa! Doo-Lang-Doo Lang-Doo-Lang

That same sliver of song wove its way into Tessa's dreams. Her tail curled. Her fingers snapped. Her head be-bobbed and her toes tip-tapped. Without opening her eyes, she waltzed toward the dancing sounds.

The rain poured down harder and harder. Oscar sang
louder and louder. *"Diddle-diddle dee-dee! Diddle
dee-dee! Doodle wop-wop! Doodle wop-wop!"*

dee-dee! Doodle wop-wop!

Tessa frolicked and frisked in time to the song.
She danced round and round until she lost her balance
and bumped into Oscar's food bowl with a clatter.

Suddenly Tessa woke up.

Oscar stopped singing. He spun toward the noise.

Cat and mouse stood staring at each other. All was quiet except for the rain on the roof.

Only one thing came to Tessa's mind. Before
Oscar could twitch a whisker, Tessa tip-tapped her
toes in time to the rain.

Oscar's mouth dropped open.

Tessa wiggled her middle to a clap of thunder.

Oscar shook his head and blinked.

Tessa burst into an all-out rock-'n'-roll, boogie-woogie, hip-hop, two-step combo.

Oscar watched, eyes wide. Finally he cleared his throat and belted out a rowdy, riotous tune just right for dancing feet.

Tessa moved to the groove. *Up, down, round and round! Jump, shout, kick it out! Swing, swoosh, shake it loose!* She felt so good she couldn't stop if she tried.

Tessa's mother crept carefully out of her hole. "Tessa, stop!" she whispered.

But Tessa couldn't hear her. She kept dancing to Oscar's song.

Then Mrs. Timboni rushed down to the kitchen in her bathrobe. "Oscar, stop!" she pleaded.

But Oscar couldn't hear her. He kept singing to Tessa's dancing.

Before long, Tessa's mother's tail twitched. She tapped her tiny toes.
Then Mrs. Timboni's throat itched. She hummed a little tune.
Soon everyone was dancing and singing along with Oscar's song.
"Doo-wang-doodle bang-doodle-doodle-doo!"
By the time the neighbors called to complain, no one
could even hear the phone ring.
And they danced—*hippy hop-hop*—and they sang—
doodle wop-wop—all night long.